MYSTERIOUS PHENOMENA

SCRIPTOR HOUSE
THE EPITOME OF GREATNESS

by Krystal Leilani Rivera Pasiliao

Scriptor House LLC

2810 N Church St Wilmington, Delaware, 19802

www.scriptorhouse.com

Phone: +1302-205-2043

Published by Scriptor House LLC

Paperback ISBN: 979-8-88692-255-4

eBook ISBN: 979-8-88692-254-7

Mysterious Phenomena

by Krystal Leilani Rivera Pasiliao

The stories I am about to tell you happened in real life and still is haunting me and my family up to this time.

My name is Krystal. I was born and raised in a small town in the Pacific Island where everybody knows almost everyone. I came from a big family of seven children. I am the third child from the youngest sibling. I have two brothers and four sisters.

I enjoyed my brothers' and sisters' company. We would go to parties together and have fun. My three sisters and I have the same height and body build. We would sometimes wear the same kind of outfits our mom sews for us. People would tell us we were like quadruplets.

Our parents were very loving and caring. Our dad was a hard-working man. He was a college professor/assistant dean at a university, and our mom was a businesswoman. She tried to help her husband send their seven children to school, and we all graduated in colleges with degrees.

We all migrated to the United States except for our youngest brother and oldest sister who chose to stay behind and settled down. Unfortunately, our oldest brother passed away here in the United States at age forty-three, and our eldest sister back home left us for-ever also at age thirty-eight. Soon our parents passed away also. When one left, the other one did not want to live anymore like to them it's the end of the world. They always wanted to be together till death. That's how much they loved each other. They were like inseparable.

Some mysterious things have been happening to our lives, and I am about to tell you in the following chapters.

CHAPTER 1

MYSTERIOUS EVENTS STARTED AT A VERY YOUNG AGE

Way back then, when we were still growing up, I already experienced some strange phenomena at a very young age. Our house was such an old one with two-story, and many of our relatives lived there and passed away after so many years. My grandma lived just across our house on a two-story building too. She always sits on a rocking chair by the window across our window also on the second floor. One day, she had gotten sick because of her old age. She was taken to the hospital. The next morning, I got up early, and I went straight to the window across her house to peak if I could see her on her rocking chair. I was so relieved to see her again sitting on the rocking chair. I immediately went downstairs to break the good news to my parents that I was so happy to see grandma better again. But I was the one who got surprised when they told me that she passed away last night. A few more years after Grandma passed away, my grandpa also passed away. My grandpa used to play ball when he was still young and active until he broke his hips and could not be operated on anymore. He lived with us, and he used a walker to get around the house. He had a rocking chair also where he always liked to sit while watching television. When he passed away, he let his presence known to us even on broad daylight. We saw his rocking chair rocking although nobody was on it. At night, we hear the sound of his walker like someone was pushing it. I slept with my eldest sister every night, and our bed is next to the window, and we always close the windows before we sleep. There is also a sheer colored hanging curtain that is half the size of the windows. The panel windows close in the middle. That same night after my grandpa died, the curtain was going up right in the middle of the windows. My sister and I covered ourselves with a blanket even though it was too hot to use a blanket. We both were so scared because we were upstairs on the second floor and that no one could do a trick like that on us. After a year had passed, our family moved and relocated to another house far from our previous house. It was just a one-story house surrounded with several fruit bearing trees. Our parents bought it from an elderly couple who could not maintain the house and all the trees around it. The house was probably as old as them.

The previous owners were about on their late eighties. I remember and will never forget when I was just about seven year old, one Saturday at night, I asked our parents if I can sleep with them because I could not fall asleep. I guess because I was in a different house, and I feel everything was new to me. It was in the middle of the night when my parents were fast asleep and soundly snoring. I could not believe it with my eyes wide open. I saw some dwarfs around me, inviting me to play with them, just like in a fairy tale, but these dwarves were quite smaller, so tiny with long beard, long hat, and wearing only ordinary old raggedy clothes. I even peaked through the windows, and I saw more dwarfs playing. I quickly woke up my dad, and when he woke up, all the dwarfs disappeared. He would not believe me when I told him about it. He said that I must be just having a bad dream or maybe I was having a fever that I was hallucinating. He then touched my forehead and neck to check if I had a fever. I was not having a fever and hallucinating nor dreaming. He did not believe me that I actually saw some dwarfs in the room.

Several years passed living in that house proved that I was not making up a story. Nobody saw the dwarfs except me, but our house-keepers experienced something else like hearing someone whistle coming deep down the ground, hearing little voices by their windows while no one was around, and lastly one of them got her foot swollen after accidentally stepping on a pile of dirt they believed was their house. She offered some fruits in front of the pile of dirt, and her swollen foot got better right after the offering. Now that I'm all grown up, and until now, I have not forgotten that night when I first saw those dwarfs.

CHAPTER 2

A SURPRISE VISIT

No matter where we go or which house we are in, something happens anywhere, anyplace. I was in my eighth month of pregnancy when we got the news from my brother back home in the Pacific Island that our eldest sister had passed away from delivering her baby. She started bleeding on her twenty-fourth week of pregnancy but decided to wait for few more weeks until her baby was in full term. That was supposed to be her second pregnancy. Her baby did not survive inside her until it was too late that her body went in shock from the toxins and bacteria from the dead fetus. She passed away from the operating room and left behind her two-year-old son and husband.

It was Mother's Day when she passed away, just one day before her birthday. When we heard the news, all of us in the United States were grieving so much. When we were growing up, she was like our mother when our mother was working. During those times, there was no internet yet, so kids go out to play with other kids. They play hide-and-seek, hopscotch, catching ball, and many other outdoor activities. But *every* time the clock turned 3:00 p.m., our eldest sister made sure that we all take a nap. Even when our parents leave out of town on a business trip, she assigned each one of us with household chores. She was very close to my youngest sister that they always share the bedroom together. They even traveled to Hong Kong together. So when she passed away, my youngest sister was so much affected, and she could not stop crying. At that time, she lived with our other elder sister in the apartment on the second floor in Los Angeles. Their living room has a big window with the view outside, and there was also a sofa besides the window. But one day on broad daylight, my sister told me that she was lying down on the sofa in the living room, facing the empty wall reflecting the sunlight coming from the window when while she was crying, she saw a shadow walked through the wall with the reflection of the sunlight. The shadow of a woman stopped right in the middle of the wall like she was looking at her. She immediately looked outside the window to see if there was a lady outside whose shadow was reflecting on the wall with the sunlight. But to her surprised, there was no one, and it would also be impossible for anyone's shadow to reflect on the wall because their apartment was way up on the second floor of the building. After she looked outside on the window and looked back on the wall, the shadow started to *leave* and then disappeared. We thought about our eldest sister that she might be just want to console her in time of our grief. Our eldest sister loved her first born so much that she could not leave in peace. She stayed as long as she can with her first born even in her spiritual body. Since her husband needed to go back to work for their son, he just left him with our brother's family to look after him.

Our aunt from our mother side of the family was also staying in our house with her adopted daughter. Her adopted daughter, who was only four years old at that time, treated her firstborn badly and unfairly. She was very naughty and mean to her first born that our deceased sister showed herself to her. Our aunt's adopted daughter got frightened to see her staring at her that she ran to her mother. Her face was so pale while she was telling our aunt whom she saw. We had no idea what happened that time, but since then, my aunt's adopted daughter stopped bullying our nephew.

Back home in the United States, a few months passed after our eldest sister's death, it was her first death anniversary to be exact that all our family gathered at home for a prayer offering for her reposed soul. Suddenly, someone rang the front doorbell three times. Everyone in the family was wondering who that could be as I got up to check and see. As I opened the front door, a cold gush of wind blew on my face as I saw no one at the door. I closed the door and went back inside to join everyone. All of a sudden, everyone felt the cold chills around the house and then silence. My father spoke and broke the silence by saying that it might be our sister in spirit who came and join us.

CHAPTER 3

GRIEF IN THE FAMILY

Life is so unpredictable sometimes. When everything is going great, one tragic accident can change it all. Our parents had been living with my youngest sister and her family in San Diego for so many years after they retired. They took care of my sister's children and kept her company while her husband was deployed. Once in a while, they would come and spend a week with my family and myself here in Los Angeles. And they also take a vacation back home overseas for at least a month.

One Sunday afternoon, something terrible happened to our parents. As they were leaving the church together with my sister and family, our mother miscalculated her step down the curb and lost her balance. While my dad was assisting her, they both fell down the curb, and she landed on our dad. My father had a bad fall as he twisted his leg, and with my mother's full weight on him, he fractured his femur. He was so much in pain while my sister's family called 911 and rushed him to the hospital.

Our father had a prostate cancer, and it was on remission when the tragic accident occurred. The surgeon gave us no choice but to let him undergo surgery right away or he will die of internal bleeding and other complications. My sister contacted everyone in the family while our dad was in the surgery room. Few days after the surgery, our dad was still in so much pain even with his new prosthetic titanium replacement of his fractured femur. He refused to walk and do his physical therapy. He became bedridden and gave up everything. It was too late when we found out that his prostate cancer metastasized throughout his body.

I was working that late afternoon when my sister from San Diego called me up on the phone and told me that our father was very critical and was dying in the hospital. She told me to come right away or I might not see him alive anymore because his blood pressure continuously declining, and he was breathing with the oxygen mask. My husband fetched me from work, and we drove straight to San Diego. When we got there in the hospital, both my sister and our mother were crying because our dad left us already. His surgery from his tragic accident prolonged his life only for six months. My sister said that our father tried to hold on for my arrival, but he could not wait any longer. He finally said goodbye just five minutes before I came. I was so devastated and cried. I really missed him. To us, he was the greatest dad on earth.

All our family and closed relatives arrived the next day when they found out that our dad passed away. My siblings and myself took care of the funeral service and dropped by the store and bought clothes for us and for our mother to wear for the funeral. Our family tradition is to wear black clothes when we are grieving in respect of the deceased relative.

We got home before lunch, and I went straight to my sister's guest room where my family and I will occupy for the night. I placed down the shopping bag with all our clothes including my mom's outfit on the chair next to my luggage. I told my sister that I will use the bathroom for a quick shower. While I was opening my luggage to get my clothes, the plastic shopping bag of clothes made a sudden movement by itself and made a sound like someone was trying to open it to see what was inside. I got startled and felt that all my hair went up and I froze. I was by myself in the room, and there was no breeze coming from the window. Suddenly, it stopped. So I continued what I was doing, and I just tried to ignore it. When I was about to close my luggage, I heard the same crisp sound of the plastic bag again, and it really sounded creepy and scary that without looking, I began running down the stairs while calling my sister.

I had a strong feeling that it was our dad trying to check the outfit we bought for Mom for his funeral. I told my sisters, and they thought the same thing. That it was our dad.

That same day in the later part of the afternoon, I tried to forget what took place in that room because I needed to do something there. I tried to remain calm and not scared. I was doing my bills in that room when suddenly there was a strong smell of roses all over the room and in the hallway. I got frightened again and quickly jumped up to my feet and ran downstairs. Dad must be there again. So I told myself that I will not be by myself anymore ever again, especially in that room.

My husband arrived that evening after he picked up our kids at home in Los Angeles. I did not mention to them about my recent experience because my kids will all get scared as well. My husband does not believe in ghosts, and he never gets scared.

It was nighttime, about eleven. When everybody went to bed, we slept in the guest room. There was a daybed and a pullout bed underneath it. My youngest son took the daybed while my husband and I slept on the pullout bed. I could not fall asleep even though I was too exhausted, and I turned off the lights. Over our head was a desk with a computer. I would guess the time was past midnight or close to one in the morning. Suddenly, I heard a movement like someone was typing on the computer, then crumpled a piece of paper, and threw it over my head. My whole body shook because of fear that I wanted to scream, but there was no voice coming out of my lips. I just cried quietly, and I did not look up to see who that could be because I was trembling in fear. I kept my eyes closed very tight thinking that my dad might be looking down at me. He continued typing, crumpled a paper again, and threw it over my head. I felt that my heart was beating so fast, and I had goose bumps all over my body. I wanted to scream and cry out loud, but I was really so scared that I froze in one position. I was lying down on my back, but I did not move at all, and I kept my eyes closed until he finally stopped. I was able to calm myself down, but I did not fall asleep at all. I was awake the whole time thinking that he might come back.

At the light of the day, I got up when everybody woke up. I was so drowsy from lack of sleep the whole night. I did not mention to anyone what took place that night because I did not like my children to hear it and be scared.

After breakfast, my husband and I were in the car heading to the funeral place to sign some papers when he started talking to me. He asked me if I heard or felt anything in our room last night like someone was using the computer and throwing a paper down to our head. "Oh my gosh!" I said. I really thought it was only me who heard and felt it. He said that he was still awake and heard it and felt everything. I was so glad that he told me that. I felt relieved that I was not alone who heard and felt that it was real and not just a dream.

That night after dinner, we had some friends and relatives who came over. My husband and brother-in-law were entertaining their friends in the patio. I overheard my husband was telling them that he woke up when someone took his blanket off him, and he actually saw the blanket lifted up in the air away from him. My husband never tells those kinds of stories ever before, and for many years of our marriage life, he never believes in ghosts until our dad died.

The day of the funeral, I woke up around five thirty in the morning to use the restroom. It was still dark outside, and everybody was still asleep. So I went back to bed and fell asleep right away because of lack of sleep the night before. Suddenly, I felt someone kicked me on my tailbone. I was so groggy that I thought my husband accidentally hit my tailbone. Then it happened again for the second time, then the third time that I woke up, and without looking, I just said stop and repeatedly said stop that hurts. I turned my back, thinking maybe it was my son, but both of my husband and son were sound asleep, and they were facing the other way. I asked myself who could that be, and if it was my dad, he must be so upset to me that I was not able to see him before his last breath.

Come breakfast time, my youngest sister got up first because she thought that I was awake already and preparing breakfast. From her bedroom, she heard someone rolling the venetian blind in the kitchen leading to the patio to open it. Then she also heard someone steering coffee in the cup. When she peaked from the hallway upstairs, everything was still closed downstairs. But she went down the stairs to prepare breakfast. She told me that Dad used to do those things every morning as soon as he gets up when he was still alive. She also said that she tried to sleep on the side of their bed near the wall so our dad won't reach her in case he comes to visit her, but with no avail, she was still smacked on her shoulder with no one in the room but her husband, who was soundly sleeping.

Our nephew who arrived late the night before slept in the living room couch. He claimed that he turned off the lights in our parent's room that night, but when he got up in the middle of the night to use the restroom, he noticed the lights were turned back on again. No one claimed going in our parent's room that night. Our mom slept in the other room with our other sister because she was scared to be alone in their bedroom. Our dad was buried at nine that morning. We missed him and loved him so much.

When our brother went back home to Pacific Island, he knew all the mysterious things that we experienced here, and after he told everyone in his family about it, nobody liked to sleep alone in their own room. So everybody set up several blankets in the living room where they can all spend the night like as if they were camping. His family was so scared that our dad will visit them also. It was true. He said at night, they could all hear our dad walking and dragging his sleepers the way he walked when he was still alive. My brother's youngest son who was only four years old that time, always slept with no blanket, but they would always see him with a blanket the next morning.

One night, my sister-in-law placed a red blanket next to my nephew before he went to sleep. It's our belief that when you wear something red or use a red blanket when you sleep, it will drive the spirit away. The spirit will not get close to you because they cannot see you. The next morning, when they woke up, my nephew was sleeping in another bed and covered with a white blanket and not red. Everyone in the family was surprised.

We had gatherings in San Diego for the prayer offering for the reposed soul of our father after a year of his death. I went to San Diego with my sister-in-law and her family also. I slept in the same room with my sister-in-law. In the middle of the night, she woke me up and asked me if I wanted to use the restroom also. Later she told me that she saw two men were inside our room. They were standing and staring at us. One was tall, and the other one was short. She looked up at them twice, and she blinked twice to make sure she was not dreaming. It was dark that she could not figure out who they were. She said they left only when she woke me up. After she told me, I could not fall asleep anymore because I got scared as well.

My sister never fails to visit our father's grave every year during his death anniversary. Several years had passed, and it was another time for my youngest sister to visit him. It happened that it was my sister's day off from work. She already bought flowers the day before after her work because she knows it was our father's death anniversary the next day. It was a cold wintery month when the day is shorter, and the night is longer. It gets dark before 5:00 p.m. My sister did all her routine household chores first like she normally does on her day off. While waiting for her laundry to get done, she was in the computer room downstairs that used to be our parent's bedroom. Suddenly, she heard footstep walking toward the computer room coming from the family room while opening a candy wrapper. She was by herself in the house. She felt like all her hair went up, but when she looked at her watch, then she realized that it was almost 3:00 p.m., and in an hour or so, it will soon get dark. Even though she got goose bumps and all hearing those weird sounds, she thought that it was just our dad reminding her to leave now before it gets dark because the cemetery closes at 5:00 p.m.

Our father even after his death still thinks that he still lives with my youngest sister. Sometimes my sister sees shadows in the corner of her eyes passing by, and sometimes she feels someone was sitting on the couch, keeping her company. Our father loved eating candies wrapped in cellophane while watching television in the family room, and he even let her know his presence by the sound of the candy wrapper. When my sister had a surgery, I stayed with her, and I looked after her. There were times that we even heard the garage door slammed without anyone at the door. The next day, her husband was gone to the store for about ten minutes when we heard his drawer closed.

We thought he came back and forgot something, but when she called him, he was still at the store. We had no idea who was that we heard. My sister consulted a priest because she thinks that our dad could not leave in peace. After the priest blessed my sister's house, it became peaceful again.

CHAPTER 4

INSEPARABLE

What is love? What is really the true meaning of love? Is there a forever in love? All these questions were lingering in my mind after the death of my father. My parents were married for sixty-four years when our dad passed away. Since then, our mother lost her will to live. Love defies death.

Since our father passed away, our mother was so devastated. She lost her appetite to eat and could not sleep well. She started getting weak and sick that she came in and out of the hospital. She was given an IV, but she kept pulling it out that her nurse tied her hands on her hospital bed. My youngest sister tried to talk some sense on her as she cried beside her. She witnessed the death of our father just few months ago, and she told her that she was not ready to go through it again with her. She made our mother promised to stay alive for her.

Our mother had emphysema, and because of her breathing difficulty, they put a tube in her throat so she can breathe. And because of this, she was placed in a nursing home. My other sister came to stay with her from morning until the end of the visiting hours. My youngest sister dropped her off before she goes to work and pick her up after work so she can also visit her. There are times that her husband picked up our other sister when she works overtime. While my sister was with our mother, our mother always looked up on the ceiling and then raises her hand like as if she was talking to someone and telling him to wait. Everyday our mother always did that, and sometimes she nodded. What my sister does, she takes our mother's hand down every time she raises it.

One day, my youngest sister told her husband not to pick up our other sister so she can visit our mother before they go to her husband's basketball game. Right after she got home, her husband arrived with our other sister. She asked her husband why he picked her up when she specifically told him not to so she can visit her. Her husband told her that she just phoned him and told him to pick her up. We were so astonished how that happened when my youngest sister did not make the phone call. So my youngest sister was not able to visit our mother that afternoon. After the basketball game, there was like about less than an hour before the visiting hours was over. My youngest sister and my other sister were both thinking of visiting her that night, but no one voiced it out to stop by the nursing home like someone was stopping them. So they just went straight home.

That same night, it was a month of June, and the weather was warm to even use a blanket. Both my sisters went to bed already by 10:00 p.m. My youngest sister felt a cold chill from her feet going up her whole body that she was shaking in coldness.

She asked her husband to grab her a comforter. Her husband was wondering why a comforter when the weather was like in low nineties. It was hot that night, and my youngest sister was not even running a fever.

She was falling asleep wrapped with a comforter when their phone rang fifteen minutes after she asked for a comforter. It was the nursing home notifying them that our mother passed away. She cried hard and immediately drove to her. Since our mother knew how devastated my youngest sister was after she witnessed the death of our father on her arms, our mother did not let her see her leave. But her spirit came to my youngest sister and hugged her to say goodbye. No wonder she felt so cold that night.

Love defies death. Now I know the true meaning of love and forever. Our parents' love lasted forever that even death would not separate them. For sixty-four years of marriage, they were inseparable and happily married. They were always together, where one goes, the other one follows. It was only six months' gap after our father's death, our mother followed him. They were buried side by side in the cemetery in San Diego.

My youngest sister never forgets their birthdays and death anniversaries and even holidays. She always visited them and offered flowers. They had a strong bond because they both lived with her, and she took care of them.

Back home in the Pacific Island, our brother's wife was telling us that while she was watching television one afternoon, she saw from the side corner of her eye a woman dressed in white, walking in their house, passing her back, and went straight to the room that used to be our parents' room. She said she even heard the door opened and closed. She wondered who that woman was who just walked in the house, so she followed her to the room. When she opened the room, she heard the bathroom closed, but when she opened the door, nobody was there. She had a feeling that our mother visited her.

Unlike our deceased father who thinks he still lived with my youngest sister, our deceased mother still thinks she still lived at home in the Pacific Island. Every night, our brother and his family always hear noises in the kitchen, but they just ignore it because they were so scared to get up and checked. And every morning when they wake up, all the pots and pans that they used the day before were all nicely stored where they belong.

Few months after her death, my husband went back home overseas to take care of some business. I was left alone with our kids at home here in the United States. One weekend, I decided to paint our kitchen. After dinner with the kids, I told them to go upstairs and I will just finish painting the kitchen. I did not realize that it was getting late, almost midnight. The streetlight went out, and the sky was hazy. It was so dark outside when I looked out in the window. Suddenly, I heard the sound of the switch on the wall of the kitchen. The lights went off like someone turned it off. It got darker inside the house that I could not see a thing in the kitchen. There were no lights in the hallway as well. I put my paintbrush down and walked toward the door to check on the switch while I bumped everything on my way, for I could not see anything. When I finally found the switch on the wall, it was not working. I tried to turn it on and off but still wouldn't work. I decided to just go upstairs and went to bed. The next morning when I got up, I checked the switch in the kitchen, and it was working fine. There was no difficulty turning the switch on and off. I phoned my sister and told her about it, and she said that maybe Mom and Dad was just telling you to stop painting because it was getting late.

One evening, I was in the kitchen at home by myself washing dishes when suddenly I heard the laundry room open. I even heard the sound of the doorknob moved. There was no breeze coming from the patio because I always make sure to close it every night, especially when I'm by myself. The laundry room is located across the kitchen. My kids were upstairs, doing their homework. I called all my son's names, thinking that one of them might have just came down. During that time, only the kitchen light was on. The hallway and the living room lights were off. No one answered when I called my kids. So I went to check the laundry room. I turned on the light there, but no one was there, so I went back to finish my dishwashing. After I finished washing dishes, I decided to do my Christmas gift wrapping. I went back to the laundry room and turned the light on. I knelt down to get the gift boxes and gift wrappers from the bottom of the cabinet. I then placed them one by one on the kitchen countertop. All of a sudden, everything on the countertop that I placed started falling off the counter when I knew I placed them right in the middle. I was so puzzled and asked myself how that could be possible unless someone pushed them to fall, but there was no one with me. So from then on, before I go to bed, I always say a little prayer for my mom. I just thought that maybe she was asking me for a prayer, and I was right because after those incidents, she never came back to visit me.

CHAPTER 5

AN EERIE SHORT TRIP

It's been awhile since I went back home in the Pacific Island. The last time I went back home was about eight years ago. Not only it takes fifteen hours long to get there, but also I have a fear of flying. All of my siblings and myself decided to travel back so we can settle our inherited property.

When the day arrived, my husband and I met all my siblings at the airport. We were all scated next to each other. It was a long flight and very uncomfortable that it was hard to stretch our legs. I had to get up once in a while. The airline was full and very noisy with babies crying. I could not even fall asleep.

We arrived at our destination at 11:00 a.m. There is a twelve-hour difference in time from the United States and there. My husband's cousin was waiting at the airport to pick us up. We stayed in a hotel just a walking distance to a big shopping mall. We actually only have to cross a bridge connected from the hotel to the mall.

It took us only a few days for us to decide what needs to be done. During our spare time, my husband rented a van so we can visit some tourist attractions in the countryside with my siblings. We stayed in in the hotel vicinity after we toured the place. We visited some close friends as well. All the places we went are all beautiful with a history of its own. We rented a cottage and had lunch by the beach. The water was very clear and calm. I could even see all the different sizes of the shells and the beautiful corals from the white sand. It was fun and nice to swim after we ate.

The following day, we visited an old lighthouse with an old wooden bed that was still intact. There were people watching over the lighthouse so they can preserve its history. There were also a couple of rooms that seem like a dining room and a bedroom. Outside the lighthouse, there is also an old deep well. It was believed that there are ghosts that are still haunting the lighthouse. The caretakers who take care of the lighthouse don't stay there overnight. They go home to their own houses and just come back in the morning to sell the tickets to get in. They are employed by the local government to keep the place well maintained. While we were there, we did not see or feel anything out of ordinary, but we took some pictures for souvenirs.

The next stop, about an hour away from the lighthouse, was a twin waterfall along the highway. It was a very long highway along the ocean view. It was a magnificent view to look at, so we stopped and took some pictures with the twin waterfall behind us.

It was a *very* long day traveling back to our brother's house. It took us at least a six-hour drive. After dinner, we were all relaxing and looking back at all the pictures that we took on our short trip. We all got shock because there was a white shadow of a man standing in the corner of the dining room in the picture. And in the bedroom on top of the wooden bed, there was a white shadow of a man and a woman lying down on it. There was no one in those rooms when we were taking pictures. We did not believe the story behind the lighthouse, but whatever was there gave us a proof. It was believed that the watchman stayed there in the lighthouse and never left it even after his wife died. We all had goose bumps.

When we looked at our other pictures where behind us are the twin waterfalls, one of the waterfalls had a huge shape of a lady holding two young boys. It was believed that the two young boys were playing on top of the waterfall when the strong current took both of them down the waterfall, and while their mother was trying to rescue them, she too fell off with them as well. It was such a sad story. Not all of us had a picture taken with the mother and the two boys. It only showed at my sister in law's camera.

CHAPTER 6

A STRANGE VISITOR

Winter season again, outside was so cold and windy. The wind was blowing everything in our backyard. A lot of leaves, papers, dirt, and even the soda cans and water bottles from the recycle bin were blown away by the wind. Our patio furniture was even being blown and hitting the wall of the house.

The heater was on inside our house. It was warm and cozy sitting on the couch by the fireplace, wrapped up with a blanket. I told my husband that I was going to stay up late and watch my favorite television shows that I recorded earlier. Everybody went to the bedroom, including my husband who decided to watch his own show in our bedroom. I must have dozed off on the couch because when I checked the time on the wall, it was almost half passed one in the morning. I was about to get up when I saw a shadow from the corner of my left eye that just sat down on the sofa next to me. I could feel that someone was sitting next to me and staring at me. I was so scared to turn my head and look. I froze. After few seconds, my husband came out of the bedroom and asked me why I was still awake at 2:00 a.m. By then,

I had the courage to look, but no one was sitting there. I told my husband about it, but he didn't believe me.

It was a long weekend the next day, so my husband and I went out of town to celebrate our wedding anniversary. We came back the following day. It was around three in the morning when we heard a loud knock on our bedroom door. Then another knock followed by another one that woke us up and asked who was there.

We thought that it might be one of our sons, but when my husband opened the door, nobody was there, and all the lights in the hallway were off. I was telling myself that hopefully my husband would believe me this time that there was really something that was visiting us because he heard the knocking at our bedroom door too.

That late afternoon, his aunt called us up and told us that his uncle passed away that morning. My husband jokingly told me that maybe it was his uncle who knocked three times that early morning.

CHAPTER 7

THE GHOST

Can ghosts be friendly or mean? Does it show up in a spirit, shadow, or bizarre shapes and sizes? My husband and I had some terrifying night experiences at home. Of all the people I know, only my husband doesn't believe in ghosts or anything supernatural until…

About a month ago later, it was in the middle of the night when I got up to use the restroom. Few minutes later, when I had fallen asleep, I woke up startled when my husband was shouting, "There is a ghost in front of me! There is a ghost! Turn on the light!" I was so scared when I heard him, so I immediately turned on the bedside lamp.

"Where is it?" I asked. I took the lamp closer to him.

"You cannot see it?" he asked. I said no. "It is still here, and look, it is now crawling up the ceiling." I did not see anything. I looked at my husband closely to make sure that he was not dreaming. He was not, and he was awake. He was looking straight to my eyes and talking to me.

Later, he said, "You can turn off the lights now, I think it's gone." After few minutes, he said, "The ghost is back. I see the ghost again. The ghost is here!"

I turned the light back on while my hands were shaking. I know my husband in so many years that I have been married to him. He was never afraid of anything like this. I took the lamp closer to him and asked him if he can tell me how it looks.

He said, "It looks like a shadow of a lady with a long white hair. I saw her crawling on the wall going up the ceiling and slowly disappearing."

I could not see anything, even a shadow, but I got goose bumps all over my body. We waited for fifteen minutes before I turned off the light again. I was not able to sleep well that night. The next morning, I asked my husband if he remembered everything that happened last night, and he said yes. He claimed he really saw a ghost, and he was not dreaming.

Year 2017, it's one of those nights when I woke up in the middle of the night. As I opened my eyes, I saw something that looks like bubblehead with two eyes staring down my husband. There were two of them. My husband was sleeping on my left side. The bubbleheads were clear and round with two eyes. Suddenly, they looked at me, and I got scared that I froze. But I kept staring at them while trying to figure out what I was seeing. I know I was fully awake and not dreaming at all. One bubblehead was slowly moving away until it disappeared, but the other one stayed. After a few seconds, it started moving slowly but toward me and then passed by me without taking its eyes off me. It stopped on my right side passed the end of the side table. It stayed watching me, and I was really getting scared because it wouldn't go away. I grabbed the crucifix on top of my side table, and I held it up against it and started praying. To my relief, it finally went away. From then on, every time I wake up in the middle of the night, I don't open my eyes anymore.

CHAPTER 8

MIRACLE

Some years ago, I celebrated my birthday in Las Vegas with my coworkers. They gave me some presents. I opened all my presents in the family room when I arrived home from Las Vegas.

One of my presents was a statue of Baby Jesus of Prague. It is holding a round ball that represents our world or mankind on one hand, and the other hand is empty but is making a sign of blessing. I wondered why the other hand is not holding a stick like what I see from the other statue of Infant Jesus. Usually, one hand has the world and the other hand has a stick. I started looking for the stick inside the box, thinking that it might have dropped while I was opening the box. When I could not find it anywhere near me and around me where all my presents were, I called my coworker, and I asked her if she remembered seeing the statue holding a stick when she bought it. She said no, and that when she saw it at the store, it was like looking at her and smiling. That's why she bought it.

After talking to her, I decided to improvise a stick. So I went upstairs to check in our bedroom if I can find something to make a stick. I found nothing, so I thought about going to our kitchen downstairs to check in the drawers in case I can use to improvise the stick. As I was going down the stairs, my last step down, I accidentally stepped on something metallic. When I looked down the shaggy carpet, there was a shiny gold metal object with a round end and the other end has a curled hook. At first, I did not know what it was and where it came from because as far as I remember, I did not drop anything like that on the carpet nor had seen anything like that before I went upstairs. When I picked it up, I had chills when I finally realized that it looked exactly like a stick of the Infant Jesus of Prague. I quickly went back to the family room, and I put it on his other hand. It fits perfectly. I felt like crying, and I started praying because I believed that I just witnessed a miracle from the Infant Jesus of Prague.

From then on, I always move the statue of the Infant Jesus of Prague from the hallway to our bedside table every night I go to sleep. I always pray the rosary to help me sleep well. I always try to stay awake until I finished praying the rosary. Until one night, when I was so tired from work and felt sleepy, I dozed off while praying the rosary. It felt like I had been sleeping for a long time while I was still in the middle part of the rosary when something woke me up. I felt the rosary was shaking my hand, and it was swaying while making a sound of the strands moving. I was not moving my hand while it was on the edge of the bed, but I was still holding the rosary, and it was moving by itself that woke me up from dozing off. It was a little dark in the room, so I used my other hand to feel the end of the rosary that has a cross so I can just do the sign of the cross and go back to sleep. When I was feeling the end of the rosary with the cross, my other hand felt that it was standing up in the air when it should be down near the floor. I suddenly opened my eyes wide, and I saw the strand of the rosary up in the air with the cross on the top. I pulled the rosary down but could not fall asleep anymore wondering about it. I just started saying my rosary again until I finished it, thinking that maybe the Infant Jesus of Prague wanted me to just finish praying my rosary. After praying, I fell asleep soundly.

After couple of years, my youngest sister was stricken with a serious health condition. My elder sister with the younger sister and myself went and stayed with her until after her surgery. We took care of her while her husband was working. I even brought with me the Infant Jesus of Prague statue, so we can all say a prayer for her to get better. Her surgery was successful, and she survived her frightful ordeal. After a couple of weeks with her, we all went back home, but I left and lend her my statue of the Infant Jesus of Prague with her. I believe in His miracle that He helped her get better.

About six months after her surgery, my youngest sister and her husband decided to come and visit me here in Los Angeles so she can also return the statue of the Infant Jesus of Prague. It takes about three to four hours to get here depending on the traffic. After traveling for couple of hours, they decided to stop by one of the fast foods on the way because it was almost time for dinner around seven at night. They parked their car near a lighted post, but it was still a little dim. My sister placed the statue of the Infant Jesus of Prague standing against the elbow rest and leaning on it to secure it. While His feet were standing securely on the containers for the soda cups right in the middle of the driver's side and front passenger's side where the hand break is.

After about half an hour, they went back to their car, but when my sister opened the front passenger door, they were amazed to see the statue of the Infant Jesus of Prague lying down on the passenger seat with His feet facing the passenger door. We really believe that He is miraculous because like any other child left behind alone in the car in a dim place, it would peak on the passenger door window and check where we at and why it was taking too long for us to come back. To make some sense out of it, we put Him down securely leaning on the elbow rest while His feet were also secured almost inside the cup container that if ever the statue accidentally fall, it will be His body first falling sideways since it's heavier, and His head should be on the passenger door. But when we saw the statue of the Infant Jesus of Prague, He was facing forward the passenger door with His feet by the door, as if He fell on His back while He was peeking on the passenger door window.

CHAPTER 9

PREMONITIONS, ONE AFTER ANOTHER

Has anyone of you ever experienced a premonition in your lifetime? I did not believe it at first until I experienced it one after another. It's such an awful feeling of experiencing something supernatural followed by bad news.

It was the night of New Year's Eve about ten thirty when my husband and I were spending the night at the casino, playing the slot machines. My husband and I were laughing hard and was having fun when suddenly I heard someone whispered to my ear that it sounded like it was coming from a deep tunnel. The words were "Mother Rosie is already dead." It was repeatedly said three times. Rosie is my husband's mother, and she lives in the Pacific Island too. The voice whispering to my ear sounded so familiar like it was her. I did not tell my husband about it that time because I was afraid that he might think that I wished his mother dead.

The next morning, we left Las *Vegas*, and we headed back home to Los Angeles. We arrived home about five in the afternoon. Our telephone answering machine was playing as soon as we opened the door. We heard my husband's brother-in-law was talking and leaving us a message asking where we at. He told us to come home in the Pacific Island because my mother-in-law passed away. That time, I was able to relay to my husband what I heard while we were in Las *Vegas.* If only I knew that what I heard was real, we could have gone home right away. Two days later, we went back home for her funeral. When we came back home after the funeral, it was a weekend when we both were still off from work, my husband and I were having coffee in the kitchen. I was sitting down at the breakfast nook, drinking my coffee while my husband was standing, looking at the newspaper. He put his coffee down close to the wall of the counter so he wouldn't knock it off while reading the newspaper. All of a sudden, his hot coffee cup started to move slowly near the edge of the counter. My husband hurriedly tried to catch it in case it falls, but I just screamed thinking that he might burn himself from the hot coffee. But to our surprise, the coffee cup stopped moving by the edge of the counter. We wondered how it happened when the counter was not even wet and slippery, and it's even flat and level. We could not think of anything that would be the reason for it but just to think that his mother came to visit us.

When I got off one afternoon, I stopped by the grocery store to pick up a can of tomato juice that I will need for our dinner. Inside the grocery store, while I was walking along the aisle of canned goods, suddenly some canned goods on the shelves started falling off. I was not even touching or getting anything yet, but the cans kept falling off the shelves one after another. I had no idea what was happening when there was not even an earthquake. I quickly ran toward the door before somebody accused me of doing all that. I was shaky and scared when I got in my car. When I reached home as I walked in the family room, our phone rang, and it was my sister who called and told me that Aunt Lucia who adopted a daughter in the Pacific Island just passed away. She was like our second mother, and she was the eldest sister of our mother. I was grieving while I was talking with my sister. I was looking out from the window when I noticed a lot of black hawks in our backyard lawn. It was so unusual to see so many hawks that day.

It was Halloween night, and I guessed all the kids were done trick-or-treating because the doorbell stopped ringing. I was sweeping the floor after dinner when I heard someone banging and hitting our front door so loud for the third time. We were not expecting any visitor that late, so we did not open the door. My oldest son's room had a huge window overlooking the front gate and the front door. When I asked him if he saw someone came in from the front gate to our front door, he said that he did not see anybody. When I asked him if he heard the banging on the front door, he said yes, and that was why he peaked at his window but saw no one.

After about half hour, the phone rang, and it was my elder sister. My heart was beating so fast because every time something like this happened, it brings bad news. As what I was expecting, my sister said that her husband already passed away. He had lung cancer, and he did not survive it. I told my sister that about half hour ago, we heard a banging on our front door three times, but no one was there. It must be my brother-in-law's spirit saying goodbye.

Years later, we moved to a new house. One night, while I was by myself watching *American Idol* on television, I made sure that all the lights on the hallway, kitchen, and living room are on. Everybody went upstairs while I was enjoying my show. About an hour or so, I felt a cold strong wind blowing my face only. I felt my bangs going up from one side of my face to the other side. I whispered, "Please stop, I'm scared." Then I started praying, and it finally stopped. I never found out what it was all about.

After about a year in our new home, my husband went back home on a short trip to the Pacific Island to take care of business. I stayed behind with our kids. After dinner, the kids went upstairs to their rooms. I also just finished doing my laundry, so I took them all up the stairs. I made sure that I turned off all the lights downstairs. While I put away the towels in the hallway cabinet just next to the stairs, I heard a loud sound of construction equipment downstairs inside the house. The sound was really coming from downstairs and not from our neighbor's house. I know there was no construction going on next door and not even at that time of the night, around eleven. I peeked outside, and all the neighbor's lights were off.

A few minutes after that, I heard a sound of flip-flop slippers being thrown or dropped from upstairs to the stairway landing downstairs. I walked from the hallway to the edge of the stairs to peek downstairs, but I did not see any slippers on the stairway landing, and no one was there. I asked my kids if anyone of them went downstairs, but they answered me no. I went downstairs myself to fix my lunch for work the next day, but everything seemed normal and quiet. I can't figure out why I still feel or hear something unusual in our new place. Everywhere I go, it seems like whatever it is follows me. Is it just my fate to experience all these unusual events?

IT RUNS IN THE FAMILY

If I could see ghosts, feel, or hear anything supernatural, my youngest sister could only feel and hear anything out of the ordinary. I heard that people like me who can see ghosts have what others call the third eye. I don't know if my sister and I can you consider lucky to be gifted. But as for me, I would rather be just an ordinary person with no such gift like this. It is such a big responsibility to be in a situation that are usually horrifying than experiencing something pleasant.

My youngest sister not only had experienced something unusual after the death of our parents and eldest sister, she also had some horrifying experience when she went back home in the Pacific Island.

It was year 2010 when she went back home with her husband and her husband's siblings for the wedding day of their niece and for their family reunion. Her husband's two older brothers still live in the Pacific Island.

After the wedding day, the newly wed went out of town for their honeymoon. All the siblings went on tour around the Pacific Island. Their first stop was a little town where her husband's brother-in-law grew up. They stayed at the brother-in-law's house. Since his parents passed away, their house became a family vacation home for all his parent's children. It has three bedrooms. My sister and her husband stayed in the room next to the bathroom. On the first night, my sister was telling me that she could already sense a presence of someone she could not see. She woke up in the middle of the night to use the restroom when she felt the chills that someone was watching them sleep.

After she used the restroom, her sister-in-law followed. Her sister-in-law has the third eye also which means she has the ability to see ghosts as well. That early morning, everyone was awake for breakfast. While they were having breakfast, they told stories of what they encountered that night in the house.

Apparently, after her sister-in-law used the restroom, she saw an elderly man walking toward the kitchen. It seemed that he just came from the living room. She noticed that he was wearing a white tank top shirt. The weather there is always tropical, very humid all the time. She did not pay much attention because she was so sleepy, and she knew that their driver was just in the living room sofa sleeping. So she just went back to her room.

They were shocked when their driver told them that there was an elderly man in white tank top shirt who was walking from the kitchen toward him. He happened to wake up when my sister used the restroom. He even heard that after my sister went back to their room, he heard the sister-in-law opened her bedroom door too. While she was in the restroom, that was the time when he saw an elderly man approaching him. He got startled to see him stopped beside him and stared at him. He was so scared that he closed his eyes again and covered himself with a blanket.

What her sister-in-law saw walking from the living room to the kitchen was apparently the deceased father of their brother-in-law. Their brother-in-law said that his father always wear a white tank top shirt in the house. And that he thinks that he still lives in the house, and he always check the new people who come and visit their house. The following day, their next itinerary was Puerto Princesa in Palawan. It is one of the favorite tourist attractions there with the famous and natural beauty of the Underground River. It was named the Seventh Wonder of the World. Anyone can fall in love with the beauty of the place.

The family checked in the hotel near the Underground River. They left their suitcase in their room, and they all went to the dock to ride a boat that will take them to the island where the Underground River is located. In the island, they have to wait for their turn to ride another boat that will take them in the Underground River. The boat can occupy up to eight people, and the guide is the one paddling the boat. The boat also has a flashlight once they get inside the cave. The Underground River is a very well protected natural wonder. The cavern has magnificent natural limestones sculptures. They all admired the wonderful and colorful stalactite and stalagmite formations.

It was already late like dinnertime when they all returned to the hotel. The hotel is big, old, and rustic but well decorated. It has its own restaurant and karaoke bar. Each family took their own room assignment on the first floor but close to one another. The first time that my sister opened their room before they left to the Underground River, she felt chills and uncomfortable because as soon as they entered, they passed the bathroom that is located beside the front door. The bathroom/restroom had brown stains all over the walls and the floor, and it had a strong smell of naphthalene that people used to kill some nasty odor or insects inside the closet, so she wondered why there were lots of them in the bathroom. The room has two queen-sized beds. My sister put their suitcase on top of the other bed with all her other souvenirs that she bought, including a big souvenir picture of them riding a cart that was being pulled by a carabao. The picture was inside a big plastic bag, so it won't get crumpled.

All the sisters settled in their room while all the guys went to the karaoke bar. My sister was by herself in the room but not too sleepy yet, so she watched the television while sitting on the other bed as she leaned on the wall. She was sitting right in the middle of their bed, and after she found the show she liked, she placed the remote beside her. Not after a short time, she was startled by three loud knocks on the wall where she was leaning. She turned her body to check what made those three knocks when there was not even a headboard and a window above the wall. She did not see a thing, so she continued watching the television when the remote control suddenly just fell on the floor. She wondered how the remote control fell off the bed when she was sitting right in the middle of the bed and the remote was just besides her.

Half an hour later, her husband came back to their room, and he was tipsy. My sister stopped watching television so her husband can rest. She turned off the lights but left the bathroom lights on. It was past midnight, while her husband fell asleep instantly, my sister still could not sleep. Something was bothering her in the room that she couldn't rest comfortably. After an hour, she was about to doze off when suddenly she heard a sound of the plastic bag where the souvenir picture was, so she got up a little bit to peek behind her sleeping husband. Her husband was sleeping at the edge of the bed next to the other bed. So his body was covering my sister's view of the other bed. When my sister peeked to see where the noise was coming from, she saw the plastic bag with the picture up in the air on top of the other bed. She opened her eyes wide and at the same time the plastic bag with picture fell on the bed. She was so scared but could not wake up her husband because he was drunk. After about half four, something *heavy* fell on the floor from the dresser. It sounded like a full big medicine bottle that was on top of the dresser that fell on the floor. Her husband who was sleeping soundly *even* heard the noise because he *moved* and lifted his head but fell back to sleep. After an hour, it must *have* been around 3:00 a.m., my sister heard something inside the closet that sounded like a marble ball rolling back and forth on the closet shelf. She was not able to sleep all night because she was so terrified. She just waited until the break of dawn.

When the sun was up, it was only 6:00 a.m., my sister got up from the bed, and when she checked the floor by the dresser, there was not *even* a medicine bottle on the floor, and when she opened the closet, it was empty and no marble balls. Her picture in the plastic bag was still on the other bed near their suitcase. She hurriedly dressed up and went straight to the front desk, and she asked to be transferred to a different room. To her astonishment, they did not *even* ask her why she likes to transfer to another room. They just *gave* her another room key from another room.

Her husband was just waking up at that time when she came back to their room. She related to him all her terrifying experiences all night. So they prepared the transfer, and after they were both ready, they met the rest of the family for breakfast in the hotel cafeteria.

My sister told her terrifying ordeal with the rest, and while she was telling the story, the waitress who was serving them was listening, and then she told them that she thought the room on top of their room is the one that is haunted. So they all figured out that all the people working in that hotel are aware of the haunting in those rooms. It was just unfortunate that they were the one who was assigned to that specific haunted room.

No wonder my sister was already uncomfortable as soon as they entered the room. She could already sense that there was something wrong because she felt her hair going up, and she had goose bumps. When she looked at the stains in the bathroom walls and floors, she already felt that someone was murdered there, and since they could not take off the smell of the murdered person's body, they just hang a lot of naphthalene scent inside the bathroom.

My sister felt nothing at the other room where they were transferred, and there was not even a single naphthalene scent anywhere. She finally had a good night sleep the following night.

It really runs in the family. My sister and I are just unfortunate to have this kind of ability to see, feel, or hear anything supernatural. It could happen to us anywhere, anyplace, and anytime. What we learned from our past experiences is to stay and be strong and to just go with the flow to keep our sanity intact. Somehow, by relating to others about our terrifying experiences, we feel relieved that we are able to release what was stuck in our mind. These terrifying incidents are not that easy to forget.

Krystal and Corazon sit before her computer. Krystal writes while Corazon surfs the internet.

KRYSTAL (V.O.) I never imagined I would ever have a normal life again. Days, weeks, and months have gone by, and my family members and I have not seen or felt anything unusual since.

CORAZON Listen to this... Krystal stops writing and looks at Corazon. She listens

CORAZON (CONT'D) (reads from the computer screen)

In reality, spirits are not something to be feared. They are simply confused and lost souls. When someone dies, they usually move on towards the light and what lies beyond. In some cases, a spirit is held back within the physical world instead of moving on. These Earthbound spirits are a form of ghosts. In reality, they are forms of trapped energy, and many do not even have a form. They do not possess the same consciousness as we do and quite often wander familiar places or stay trapped within their home or an item that is precious to them. In some cases, these spirits aren't even aware they are dead. In others, they are confused and don't understand what has happened to them or where to go. This is why helping the Earthbound spirits cross over is vitally important.

ONE YEAR LATER

INT. NEW HOME 1 - DAY It is a cloudy morning. Krystal enters the living room with a steaming cup of coffee. She sits down before the TV and watches the morning news. Suddenly, she hears the side gate open but pays little attention. Through the corner of her eye, she sees a MAN'S SHADOW pass outside the first window covered with a clear curtain. She turns to the window and sees Man's Shadow pass by the second curtain. She waits expectantly to know who the person is but hears no knock. Still sitting on the couch, Krystal looks into the backyard but sees no one there. She looks again and sees Man's Shadow standing behind her and looking down at her. She quickly looks away and freezes with her eyes wide open.

Krystal (V.O.) Is this the beginning of a new phenomenon?

ABOUT THE AUTHOR

Krystal Leilani Rivera Pasiliao is a registered nurse, graduated with a bachelor's degree in nursing. She is specialized in various fields of nursing, such as Emergency Room, Critical Care & Employee Health/Occupational Health Nursing.

Although she is new to this kind of profession, she finds it is not difficult to create a story because they are true to life stories based on her past & present experiences. This is her second time to write a book, following her first book "What Made Me Love My Profession," a collection of true stories that have occurred during her nursing career.

Krystal's inspiration in writing this book of phenomena is something unimaginable, and maybe some would say impossible, but actually happened in her real life.